The Thanksgiving Surprise

Originally published as *Turkey Surprise*

The gopher hole

The pond

The Thanksgiving Surprise

Originally published as *Turkey Surprise*

Peggy Archer

illustrated by **Thor Wickstrom**

SCHOLASTIC INC.
New York   Toronto   London   Auckland   Sydney
Mexico City   New Delhi   Hong Kong   Buenos Aires

Two pilgrim brothers sang as they walked down the path together.

"We're two mighty pilgrims
coming your way.
Looking for a turkey
for Thanksgiving Day.
We'll pluck him, and stuff him,
and cook him up right.
We'll gobble, gobble turkey
for dinner tonight!"

The little pilgrim thought about plucking and stuffing. He thought about cooking.

He wasn't so sure about plucking and stuffing and cooking.

He wasn't so sure about having a turkey for Thanksgiving dinner.

"The first turkey we see will be Thanksgiving dinner," said the big pilgrim.

The little pilgrim looked through his spyglass. "But what if we don't *see* any turkeys?" he asked.

"Don't worry," said the big pilgrim. "We will."

Around the bend, a turkey was in a tizzy! "The pilgrim brothers are coming!" he cried. "If they see me, they'll pluck out all my feathers, stuff me with bread crumbs, and cook me for Thanksgiving dinner. Where, oh where, can I hide?"

"Turkey," a bird called, "fly up here in this tree. The leaves will hide you."

He flew up into the tree.

He flapped his wings.

The turkey took a running start.

Then, *Whoosh!* A breeze climbed into the air. It blew the dry leaves right off the tree.

"Oh, no," cried the turkey. "Here come the pilgrim brothers!"

The little pilgrim looked through his spyglass. He saw a tree with its leaves on the ground. He saw something in the tree.

"I'm tired of turkey for Thanksgiving dinner," the little pilgrim said. "Are you *sure* we want a turkey?"

"Well," the big pilgrim said, "*Father* wants a turkey."

"Come on," the little pilgrim said. "Let's go this way." And off they went in another direction, singing:

"We're two mighty pilgrims
coming your way.
Looking for a turkey
for Thanksgiving Day.
We'll pluck him, and stuff him,
and cook him up right.
We'll gobble, gobble turkey
for dinner tonight!"

The turkey ran the other way. He saw a gopher sitting in the grass.

"The pilgrim brothers are coming!" the turkey cried. "If they see me, they will pluck out all my feathers, stuff me with bread crumbs, and cook me for Thanksgiving dinner. Where, oh where, can I hide?"

"You can hide in a hole in the ground like me," the gopher said.

He jumped into his gopher hole. The turkey dove in after him.

His head went in. His neck went in. But the rest of him would not go in.

"Oh, help," cried the turkey. "I'm stuck! Now what will I do?"

"Don't worry," said the gopher. From inside his gopher hole, he pushed and pushed.

Pop! The turkey fell backward onto the ground.

"Oh, dear!" cried the turkey. "Here come the pilgrim brothers!"

The little pilgrim looked through his spyglass. He saw a gopher hole. He saw something sitting next to the gopher hole.

"I never really liked turkey," the little pilgrim said. "Are you *really* sure we want a turkey for Thanksgiving dinner?"

"Well," the big pilgrim said, "*Mother* wants a turkey."

"Come on," the little pilgrim said. "Let's go this way." And off they went, in a new direction, singing:

"We're two mighty pilgrims
coming your way.
Looking for a turkey
for Thanksgiving Day.
We'll pluck him, and stuff him,
and cook him up right.
We'll gobble, gobble turkey
for dinner tonight!"

The turkey ran the other way. He came to a pond. A fish was swimming in circles.

"Oh, Fish!" the turkey cried. "The pilgrim brothers are coming. If they see me, they will pluck out all of my feathers, stuff me with bread crumbs, and cook me for Thanksgiving dinner. Where, oh where, can I hide?"

"You can hide behind this rock, like me," said the fish. "See? Just jump into the water."

 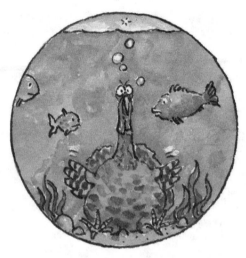 

The turkey jumped into the water. *Plop!*

He sank to the bottom of the pond.

Gurgle, gurgle went the water into his eyes and nose.

Cough, cough went the turkey as he pushed himself up.

Splutter, splatter went the water out of the turkey's nose and mouth.

"I just remembered," he said to the fish. "Turkeys can't swim!

And here come the pilgrim brothers!"

The little pilgrim looked through his spyglass. He saw a pond. He saw something big and wet beside the pond.

"Turkey, turkey, turkey," the little pilgrim said. "Is that all anyone has for Thanksgiving dinner?"

"Well, no," the big pilgrim said. "There's corn on the cob, and applesauce, and dessert, too. But Mother and Father want us to bring home a turkey."

"Well," said the little pilgrim. "What if we can't *find* a turkey?"

The big pilgrim thought. "Well, we have to bring *something* home," he said.

The little pilgrim looked through his spyglass again. "I'll meet you at the pumpkin patch," he said.

The big pilgrim went to the pumpkin patch. The little pilgrim went to the pond. He came face-to-face with the turkey.

"Come on!" he said to the turkey. "You can hide behind the woodpile, like I do."

The turkey trembled.

"Quick," said the little pilgrim. "Before my brother sees you!"

The turkey ducked behind the woodpile. The little pilgrim smiled.
He went to find his brother.

"What a good Thanksgiving dinner we will bring home!" he said.

The two pilgrim brothers walked down the path together. They carried a heavy pumpkin between them. They sang,

"We're two mighty pilgrims
coming your way.
Bringing home a feast
for Thanksgiving Day.
Turkey sounds good
all stuffed with bread.
But we'd rather gobble, gobble
pumpkin pie instead!"

To Chuck, and all the gobblers who followed—
Kathy, Brian, Kevin, Dan, Megan, and Sarah
—P. A.

To my Scandinavian brothers, Matti and Lennart
—T. W.

Originally published as *Turkey Surprise*

ISBN-13: 978-0-545-05929-9
ISBN-10: 0-545-05929-1

12 11 10 9 8 7 6 5 4 3   7 8 9 10 11 12/0

Printed in the U.S.A.   08

First Scholastic printing, November 2007

Designed by Jasmin Rubero

Text set in Bookman

Pilgrim brothers' house

The tree

The pumpkin patch

The woodpile

The gopher hole

The pond

Peggy Archer is the author of *Turkey Surprise* and *From Dawn to Dreams: Poems for Busy Babies*. In addition to her writing, she works as a medical and pediatric nurse, and as a substitute school nurse. She first came up with the idea for *Turkey Surprise* when she learned that wild turkeys could fly. Archer lives with her husband in Indiana.

Thor Wickstrom has illustrated many picture books, including *School Picture Day*, *Teacher Appreciation Day*, *Pajama Day*, and *Book Fair Day* (by Lynn Plourde). He is also the illustrator of the Easy-to-Reads *Chickie Riddles* and *Puppy Riddles* (by Katy Hall and Lisa Eisenberg). Like the little pilgrim, Wickstrom enjoys pumpkin pie and vegetarian "tofurkey" with his family on Thanksgiving. He lives in Massachusetts.